Dear Parent:

Christmas is a special time for many people and Arthur the Aardvark is no exception. Like many youngsters his age, Arthur takes holidays very seriously. He puts a lot of time, effort, and thought into what gift to give Santa Claus. Arthur knows that the spirit of giving is what really counts.

The holidays are perfect for sharing and so we'd like to share with you a few helpful hints about reading:

❄ **Obtain a library card for your child.** Let your child choose his or her own books.

❄ **Be sure your child has books when you are on a long trip or when you're waiting in a doctor's office.**

❄ **Make reading a habit.** Plan a special (and regular) story time—just after dinner or before bed time.

Marc Brown, the author/illustrator of the Arthur series (there are now more than 12 books) says, "Books are my way to celebrate what is wonderful!" We hope that *Arthur's Christmas* adds to your holiday celebration.

Sincerely,

Fritz J. Luecke
Executive Editor
Weekly Reader Books

Weekly Reader Children's Book Club Presents

ARTHUR'S CHRISTMAS

MARC BROWN

Little, Brown and Company

BOSTON TORONTO LONDON

This book is a presentation of Weekly Reader Books. Weekly Reader Books offers book clubs for children from preschool through high school. For further information write to: **Weekly Reader Books,** 4343 Equity Drive, Columbus, Ohio 43228.

Published by arrangement with Little, Brown and Company. Weekly Reader is a federally registered trademark of Field Publications.

Third Printing

Library of Congress Cataloging in Publication Data

Brown, Marc Tolon.
  Arthur's Christmas.

  "An Atlantic Monthly Press book."
  Summary: Arthur puts a lot of time, effort, and thought into his special present for Santa Claus.
  [1. Gifts—Fiction. 2. Christmas—Fiction.
3. Santa Claus—Fiction. 4. Animals—Fiction]
I. Title.
PZ7.B81618Aol 1984   [E]   84-4373
ISBN 0-316-11180-5
ISBN 0-316-10993-2 (pbk)

JOY STREET BOOKS
ARE PUBLISHED BY
LITTLE, BROWN AND COMPANY (INC.)

WOR

*Published simultaneously in Canada
by Little, Brown & Company (Canada) Limited*

PRINTED IN THE UNITED STATES OF AMERICA

For my Grandma Thora,
who taught me about giving

Arthur and D.W. had been in the drugstore a long time.
"For heaven's sake," D.W. said. "This store is full of presents. Pick one and let's go!"

"It has to be just right," said Arthur. "I want Santa to like it."

"Well, hurry up," said D.W. "I want to get home and see if Grandma's there and how many presents she brought me."

At home, D.W. added ten more things she wanted to
her Christmas list and copied it over in red pencil.
Arthur and D.W. cheered when they heard the car
in the driveway.
"Grandma, are there presents in there for me?"
asked D.W.

"Grandma, do you think Santa would like new mittens or gloves?" asked Arthur.
"Whatever happened to, 'Hello, I'm glad to see you'?" asked Grandma Thora.

GOOD DOG

After dinner, everyone relaxed.

"Look," said D.W. "I teached Killer a trick."

"Taught," said Grandma. "You taught Killer a trick."

But D.W. didn't hear. She had seen something on
television to add to her list.

"Arthur, what's the matter?" asked Grandma.

"I haven't found the right gift for Santa,"
said Arthur.

"Only two shopping days left," reminded D.W.

The next day, Arthur, D.W., and their friends went shopping. Killer went, too.

Arthur searched the entire store and still couldn't find the perfect gift for Santa.

"What's the big problem?" asked D.W. "I can see a hundred things I want. Let's go tell Santa."

"Santa, what would *you* like for Christmas?" asked Arthur.

"Ho, ho, ho," laughed Santa. "You just leave the giving to me."

D.W. had her picture taken patting Santa's tummy.

Buster was next.

"Santa, be careful coming down the chimney at our house. My parents always forget to put out the fire."

"Ho, ho, ho," said Santa. "Don't worry. I'll use the front door."

Then it was Francine's turn.

"Have you been a good little girl?" asked Santa.

"Oh, yes," smiled Francine. "I'm always good."

"Always?" asked Santa.

Afterward, Buster treated them all to ice cream.
Arthur could hardly finish his root beer float.
He had only one more shopping day.
"Look!" said Francine. "Santa eats ice cream!"
"I'll have a banana split with six scoops of bubble
gum ice cream," said Santa.
"With double hot fudge, whipped cream, and nuts."
"I'll say he eats ice cream," said D.W.

At home, Arthur asked his family for help.
"How about a nice colorful tie?" said Father.

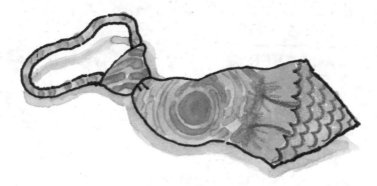

"After-shave is always a good gift," said Mother.

"I bet Santa could use some toasty-warm
long johns," said Grandma.

That afternoon, everyone was getting ready
to go caroling.
But Arthur didn't have time for Christmas carols.
Time was running out.
"Please come along," begged D.W. "I'll be the
only kid. And besides, Mrs. Tibble always
gives us a present and hot chocolate."

Arthur went window shopping instead, hoping that would give him an idea for Santa's present. Santa was Ho-ho-ho-ing and drinking a diet root beer at the car wash.

Moments later Santa was at the Golden Chopstick, eating subgum chow goo.

Santa must have run to the deli at the corner
of North and Main.
The waitress shouted Santa's order to the cook.
"Catch a fish, hit it with rye, and put
a pair of shoes on it!"
"Santa sure eats a lot," thought Arthur.

Finally Arthur went home.
He hadn't seen a single thing in any of the
store windows he thought Santa would like.
Santa was on TV eating Papa Piper's
pickled peppers.
"That's it!" said Arthur.
He started making his list.

Arthur counted his money.
"D.W.," he said in his sweetest voice.
"Okay, how much do you need?" asked D.W.
"But only if you promise to stop being
such a grouch."

The next morning, Arthur gave D.W. half of his list. He took the other half.

D.W. had to keep Killer out of the kitchen
while Arthur made Santa's present.
"What's all that noise?" asked Father.
"Arthur is making a mess," reported D.W.
The kitchen door opened, and Arthur sneezed.
"Mom, how many cups of pepper in pickled
peppers?" he asked.
"Maybe I should help," said Mother.
"No, please," said Arthur. "I want to make
Santa's present myself. Just tell me
how many sticks of gum in subgum chow goo?"
"Poor Santa," said D.W.

Hours later, Arthur whistled while
he set the table for Santa.
"What's *that?*" asked Father.
"Pickled peppers, a hot fudge sundae on
bubble gum ice cream, and subgum chow goo.
I sort of combined Santa's favorite
foods," Arthur explained.

"What's that big lumpy thing that's moving?"
asked Grandma.
"A pizza to go," said Arthur. "With
everything on it."
"If you want Santa to come, you'd better
go to bed," said Mother.
"If we want Santa to come," thought D.W.,
"we'd better do something about that food."

D.W. couldn't fall asleep.
"I have to do something," she thought. "Poor Arthur worked so hard. But if Santa gets one whiff of Arthur's present, he'll never set foot in the dining room—much less eat any of it." Careful to miss the squeaky step, D.W. tiptoed downstairs in the dark.

The next morning,
Arthur was the first one up.
"Santa ate it all!" he cried.
"And he left a note!"